G.I. DOGS

PRISONER
OF WAR

JUDY

Other books by

LAURIE CALKHOVEN

Military Animals

Women Who
Changed the World

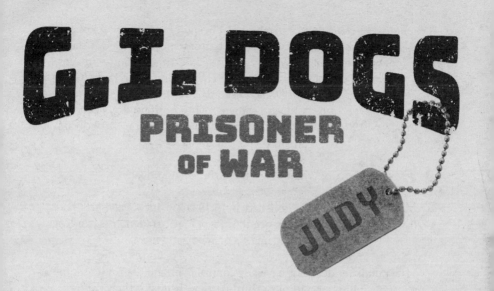

G.I. DOGS
PRISONER
OF WAR

JUDY

Laurie Calkhoven

Scholastic Inc.

Copyright © 2018 by Laurie Calkhoven

Library of Congress Cataloging-in-Publication Data available

ISBN 978-1-338-18523-2

10 9 8 7 6 5 4 3 2 1   18 19 20 21 22

Printed in the U.S.A.   40
First edition, April 2018

Book design by Baily Crawford

For the people and animals around the
world whose lives are disrupted by war.
May you find peace.

PROLOGUE

ESCAPE FROM
SINGAPORE

Singapore was under siege. As a ship's dog on the HMS *Grasshopper*, an English gunboat, my job was to keep the men's spirits up and warn them when danger was near. Today, danger was all around.

Japanese bombs had been falling since December. The first Japanese troops entered Singapore in February 1942. On the eleventh, the British got the order to evacuate. Soldiers, government workers, and British and Chinese families all crowded the pier, fighting for a place on a ship—any ship. Every vessel, from small fishing boats to private yachts and passenger steamers, no matter how old, was called into service.

Gunfire and bombs were all around us. The normal waterfront smells mingled with the unsettling scents of smoke and death. And underneath all the other smells was fear. The civilians, especially the children, were terrified, and it was my job to help them. I was afraid, too, but I never let them see it.

On February 13, the final evacuation began. Sailors desperately tried to keep order on the pier while confused and frightened mothers and children came on board the *Grasshopper*. My friend George White gave each person a cup of tea and a piece of chocolate, while I wagged my tail, nuzzled little fingers, and barked a hello.

Welcome to the Grasshopper, I told them. *You're safe here.*

As darkness fell, we began to pull out of the crowded harbor, when suddenly we got the order to turn around. There was another group of refugees who needed to come on board. Every inch of the ship was already full, but we somehow made room for more.

We finally left the harbor after midnight. The hardest thing was hearing the shouts from the people who had been left behind. I stood on the deck and howled with them.

I'm sorry. We're already dangerously overcrowded. There's no more room.

As soon as we were out of earshot, I snuggled down between two of the most frightened children and tried to get some sleep. But, as always, my ears were on alert for the sound of Japanese warplanes and the bombs they carried.

With luck, we'd make it to Java in a few days, and from there, larger ships could take us to India or Australia.

Unfortunately, luck wasn't on our side.

I'm going to tell you the story of how I became an official Japanese prisoner of war during World War II, and how I managed to keep myself and my men alive.

But before we get to all that, let's start at the beginning—in Shanghai, China.

CHAPTER 1

ADVENTURE IN SHANGHAI

It all started at the Shanghai Dog Kennels in Shanghai, China, in February 1936. My mother was one of the finest English pointers in the city, and I looked just like her. My face was almost entirely brown and my body was white with lots of brown spots. I was born in the English-run dog kennels, which meant that as soon as I was big enough, one of the English families living in Shanghai would bring me home.

The English loved Chinese tea, silk, and other goods, so there were a lot of English people living in the country at that time, working for companies that shipped those goods back to Great Britain. They tried hard to make

China feel like home, which included having dogs as pets. Pointers are very playful, especially with children, and we also make great gundogs.

Gundogs *point* to game when their humans are hunting. We're much better at that than humans could ever be. To be perfectly honest, human noses don't work very well. That's why humans need dogs. My sense of smell is about a hundred thousand times more powerful than yours.

At three weeks old, I was at the kennel, waiting for my real life to begin. I was ready for adventure and tired of being kept in a cage. The excitement of Shanghai was just a few feet away—rickshaws, cars, bicycles, food carts, horseflies, shops, and people. Best of all were the smells— so many of them! And I wanted to investigate them all. So when no one else was looking, and my brothers and sisters were busy crowding around my mom, I wiggled my nose under the wire. Then I wiggled some more. And then I popped right through the wire fence and onto the street.

It was amazing! I ran from one smell to the next, checking everything out, dodging rushing feet and rolling tires. A fly landed on my nose and took off. I chased it, but it was too fast for my pudgy little legs. A few people stopped to pet me, but a food cart vendor gave me a shove when I tried to check out his wares.

That made me realize I was hungry, and it was starting to get cold, too. I was ready to go home, but I couldn't remember where home was. I had dashed here and there, from one smell to the next, without paying any attention.

What am I going to do?

I whimpered, hoping someone would stop and help. No one did.

I lifted my nose and sniffed a big sniff, hoping to follow the scent of the kennels—the warm, delicious smell of puppies and my mother and the humans who took care of us. But there were too many other smells crowding around me.

I was lost. I was scared. I was cold. But mostly I was hungry.

I have to fill my belly, I realized. *Then I can find home.*

So I searched for food.

Garbage heaps turned out to be the best place to find a snack, and once in a while a nice human slipped me a handful of rice. Even so, I could never fill my belly and I never did find home. Days went by, and then a week or two. I was hungry all the time.

I wandered around the city, searching for food and a cozy place to live. Not all of the humans I ran into were nice, and I started to think I would never find a safe place. Then I found Mr. Soo standing by the back door of his shop.

"Hello there," he said, reaching down to pet me. "You look hungry, little one."

I trained my big brown eyes on him and wagged my tail to say, *I'm hungry and I like you.*

Mr. Soo went back inside, and I was afraid that he wouldn't come out again. But he did! And he had food! He gave me a small handful of rice and fish from his lunch.

I learned that not only did Mr. Soo love dogs, but he also had a small store full of all kinds of interesting things. He sold stuff mostly to the British and American sailors that were all over Shanghai.

At that time, Shanghai was full of westerners. It's a port city on China's coastline that sits at the mouth of the Yangtze River—Asia's longest river. England, America, and France all had business in the country. But because warlords and pirates sailed the Yangtze, those countries sent gunboats to patrol the waters and keep their merchant ships safe.

I stayed with Mr. Soo for a few weeks after that. He fed me scraps of his own meals every day, and he let me sleep in a box in the alley behind his shop. Sometimes he let me in the store and I helped him wait on the sailors. Mr. Soo saved my life. Shanghai was a dangerous place for a dog like me, and I was safe in his shop. I still patrolled the neighborhood looking for extra scraps, but I was grateful to have a box to sleep in and a kind human to visit every day.

I thought that might be my life from then on. But another danger made itself known—Japanese sailors.

Japan's ships, like England's and America's, sailed up and down the Yangtze River. Japanese sailors patrolled Shanghai, and often got into fights with the English and

Americans. I had learned to recognize Japanese sailors pretty quickly after I escaped from the kennel—mostly because they always kicked me. And tonight there was a whole group of them yelling and throwing things around in Mr. Soo's shop.

Mr. Soo tried to get them to stop. When he did, they started to hit him. He was already on the floor, bleeding, when I ran through the back door into the shop. The Japanese sailors knocked over shelves, breaking everything and then stomping on the pieces. I tried to run to Mr. Soo's side, but the sailors spotted me. One gave me a kick and another threw something at my head. Then a third one grabbed me by the neck and carried me outside.

I yelped, partly because I was in pain and partly to attract attention, but no one had time to come to my rescue. That sailor kicked me across the street and into a pile of garbage. I heard them all laughing as they left the shop.

Neighbors ran to help Mr. Soo, but no one saw me or came to help. My stomach hurt and I was scared. I was afraid someone would come along and step on me. So I limped into an empty doorway and curled up.

It was dark. I shivered and cried from the cold and the fear and the pain while I watched the sky slowly change from black to purple to pale gray. I sniffed the air around me, hoping for the smell of food or Mr. Soo. But instead, there was another smell I recognized—Lee Ming!

Lee Ming's mother worked with Miss Jones, the English lady in charge at the Shanghai Dog Kennels. The little girl used to come and visit and play with my brothers and sisters and me. I liked her.

I lifted my snout to smell her good, friendly smell, and I started to cry harder in the hope that she would hear me. The next thing I knew, she was kneeling in front of me. Even with just a human nose, she recognized me right away.

"*Shudi!* Oh, Shudi, where have you been?" Lee Ming asked.

I tried to thump my tail as a way to say *hi* and *I've missed you* and *Japanese soldiers are mean*, but I hurt too much.

Lee Ming picked me up gently and wrapped me in her raincoat.

I'd had no idea I was so close to the kennels and regular meals all this time, but we were home in minutes. She brought me straight to Miss Jones.

"Look who I found!" Lee Ming said.

"Goodness! Is that our missing pointer?" Miss Jones asked. Then she said wonderful, wonderful words: "I think we should give her a bath and a good dinner."

They got no argument from me. Although I would have changed the order of things and had a good dinner first and *then* the bath.

Lee Ming and Miss Jones were very gentle. They cleaned me up, fed me, and made sure I wasn't seriously hurt.

Lee Ming could tell I didn't like all the poking and prodding. She wrapped me in a blanket and held me in her arms. I stayed awake only long enough for them to make my name official.

"You're okay; there, there, little Shudi," Lee Ming said.

"Why did you call her Shudi, Ming?" Miss Jones asked.

"*Shudi* means 'peaceful,'" Ming told her. "Look at her. Doesn't she look peaceful?"

"She does," Miss Jones said. "Then that will be her name—Judy."

So from then on, I was called Judy. And it wasn't long before I was back to my old self—plump, shiny, and ready for fun. My mother and my siblings had all gone on to their humans' homes, but there were other dogs for me to play with and warn about the dangers in the outside world.

Stay away from Japanese sailors, I warned them. *And anyone with hungry eyes.*

We all agreed that eating dogs was a horrible, no-good thing to do.

Luckily, we were all in a place with humans who loved dogs and would make sure we went to good homes. Now that I was healthy and well-fed again, I began to wonder what mine would be like.

I was almost six months old when my next adventure began, but I didn't escape the kennels again. This time I was *chosen*.

Remember I said that English gunboats patrolled the Yangtze River? The *Gnat* was one of those ships. And it was nearly perfect. There was just one thing missing—a mascot. So while the ship was docked in Shanghai to get fixed up and collect supplies, Lieutenant Commander J. M. G. Waldegrave (the ship's captain, called a "skipper") and Chief Petty Officer Charles Jeffery set off for the Shanghai Dog Kennels to find one.

They had three requirements. There were only men on the ship, so they wanted a girl to balance things out. They wanted that girl to be a beauty. And they wanted a dog that was able to earn her keep.

Jeffery took one look at me and let out a slow whistle. You can't blame him. I'm a beautiful pointer, so they thought I would make a good hunting dog. I already liked Jeffery's smell, and when I heard him whistle, I jumped right into his arms. The next thing I knew, I was an official member of the British Royal Navy.

That very afternoon, I went to live on the HMS (short for His Majesty's Ship) *Gnat*. Like other gunboats, the *Gnat* was small and fast and able to maneuver in the

Yangtze. She had some big guns on her deck and even a couple of antiaircraft cannons.

The skipper and the chief petty officer brought me aboard and hid me in a small room with a quartermaster. Then I heard someone say, "All hands on deck in ten minutes!"

Sailors pulled on their uniforms and crowded onto the deck.

One of them, a first lieutenant, climbed onto a wooden crate and made an announcement about how shooting parties going ashore to hunt would have to come back with more than just one duckling in the future.

He turned and yelled, "Quartermaster!"

The quartermaster led me out onto the deck.

There were a few whistles and then a big cheer. I gave all the sailors my biggest smile while I wagged my tail.

"Here she is, gentlemen," the first lieutenant said. "Meet the first lady of the gunboats—Judy RN."

That's short for Royal Navy. I was official!

I raised my snout and tried to look as first-lady-ish as possible, but it's hard to look dignified when you're as happy as I was at that moment. I had an exciting new life in front of me. One that was going to be full of adventure, nice humans, and—most important—food!

Able Seaman Jan "Tankey" Cooper was named the "Keeper of the Ship's Dog." Tankey was in charge of the ship's food and freshwater tanks. He was also the ship's butcher, which meant lots of bones for me. I loved Tankey, but really I belonged to the whole ship.

It wasn't long before I knew every nook and cranny on the *Gnat* and every sailor, too. It was a good life. I had plenty of chow and lots of juicy bones. There was always someone around to play with. And if I didn't feel like sleeping in my comfy blanket-filled box on the ship's deck, I could always curl up with one of the sailors.

The skipper and the chief petty officer, along with Tankey, did their best to train me "for the gun." When they took me on shore, I was supposed to go rigid and point whenever I scented a duck, quail, antelope, or gazelle in the woods around the Yangtze. Well, it turned out I wasn't very good at that. I was only good at pointing at one thing—the ship's galley when dinner was being cooked.

By the time the HMS *Gnat* left Shanghai in November 1936, everyone accepted that I was a ship's dog and not a gundog. My training started too late for me to be able to learn that now. I'd have to prove myself useful in other ways—if my curiosity didn't get me into trouble first.

CHAPTER 2

DOG OVERBOARD!

I was used to the noise of Shanghai, but the roar of the *Gnat*'s engines and the rush of the water as we fought our way upstream was another thing entirely. The gray foam that followed the ship, churned up by the engines, fascinated me. So did the yellowish-brown water that stretched in front of us. It was full of new smells.

A few days after I joined the ship, I wiggled under the ship's rail and onto the steel plates on the outer edge of the deck to get an even closer look. I had seen men out there before. They always attached themselves to the rail with a leash.

As soon as I got out there, I realized why. *These steel plates are wet and slippery!*

I danced around, barking at the churning, frothing water below me and trying to keep my footing.

The last thing I heard as I went over the edge was "Man overboard! No! Dog! Dog overboard!"

I hit the water with a giant splash and howled. Bad-tasting water rushed into my mouth.

This is cold! And deep!

I had splashed in puddles and in baths, but I had never been in deep water before. I paddled and paddled, trying to keep my head above water.

Even worse than the deep, cold water—the *Gnat* was going in one direction and the rushing river was carrying me in the other! I paddled as hard as I could, but there was no way I'd be able to fight my way back to my ship. The water was too rough and too fast.

I'm in big trouble!

Suddenly, there was a buzzing sound behind me. I couldn't see what it was over the choppy water, but it got louder and louder as I struggled to keep myself from being dragged under.

Then I saw it—a small boat with Seaman Vic Oliver at the tiller. He fought his way toward me, and then he passed right by. One of the Chinese boat boys and another seaman were with him.

I would have barked to say, *Come back!* but keeping my head above water took every bit of energy I had.

Then Oliver gave the boat a tight turn. The Chinese boat boy leaned over the side to grab my collar.

Rescue! I thought.

But not quite—the boy fell overboard, too, and we were both dragged under! I could feel him thrashing near me while I fought to break the surface and take a breath. The next thing I knew, two sets of hands were pulling me, and then the boy, out of the water.

I heard a cheer from the deck of the *Gnat* as I slumped, shivering, in the bottom of the rescue boat. When I got back on ship, I was covered in Yangtze River mud. I thought I smelled wonderful, but CPO Jeffery insisted on giving me a hot bath, which was fine since I was freezing.

Then he took me back out on deck. That scared me a little—I didn't want to fall overboard again! But he pointed to all the things I should stay away from, and that included anything too close to the edge.

Believe me, I thought, *I'm never going to do that again.*

My usual habit was to wander around the ship at night and choose a place to sleep, but that night I stuck close to the CPO. I needed a peaceful rest after all the excitement.

The next few days were exactly that—peaceful. We steamed along upriver, waving to French and British ships going the other way. I curled my lip and growled when four Japanese warships passed by us. I recognized their uniforms. And their flag.

Kickers, I thought.

We pressed on until we passed Nanking, China's capital, and reached a small settlement called Wuhu. That meant expeditions on shore. There was a Navy canteen that served ice cream, and let me tell you, it was delicious!

Too soon we continued upriver, into a land of steep

gorges. The walls towered above us on either side of the river. One night, far from any settlement, we were forced to lay anchor in one of those wild, unpopulated gorges. There was no sign of danger, but I slept on deck anyway— just in case. Something told me to be on the alert.

Around three o'clock in the morning, I heard something that wasn't right. I shrugged off my blanket and sat up.

There it was again. A quiet, sneaky noise.

Living on the streets of Shanghai had taught me about danger and how to sense when it was near. I knew something threatening was coming toward us.

Pirates!

Human ears are about as useful as their noses. I knew the officer on watch didn't hear the danger, so I started to bark.

He tried to shush me. "Quiet, girl, you'll wake everyone up."

I'm not stopping until you pay attention, I barked.

Thankfully, he did. He directed a signal light in the

direction I was pointing and trained it on the river. Finally, he saw what was coming—two large pirate junks, or flat-bottomed boats, drifting silently toward us.

Not so silently that my super-powerful ears didn't hear you, I thought.

Now that he saw the danger, I did what the watch officer asked and shushed.

Won't those pirates be surprised when they try to board the ship!

The officer fired one shot into the sky. Within seconds the *Gnat*'s deck was full of pajama-wearing sailors ready to fight. It would have been a funny scene if real danger wasn't heading right toward us.

The pirates weren't as smart as me. Either they didn't know they had been spotted or they were too far into their criminal plan to turn back. The junks came along either side of the *Gnat*, snagging us in the long bamboo rope that stretched from one of the pirate vessels to the other.

The minute that rope hit our prow, the *Gnat*'s machine

guns opened fire. Even so, the shadowy figures rose up and tried to board our ship, only to be met with more gunfire.

Now I felt perfectly free to bark and snarl at a pirate who jumped onto our deck.

He froze and backed up.

Be afraid, I warned him. *Be very afraid.*

Some of the *Gnat*'s sailors chopped away at the rope that was meant to trap us between the two pirate ships. As they broke through, the junks slipped into the darkness, pulled by the fast-moving current. The pirate under my watch jumped into the river to try to catch his ship.

I've been in that water, I thought. *You're not going to make it.*

When it was all over, we celebrated our victory. Tankey gave me a bone he had been saving for a special occasion and the watch officer made sure everyone knew that I had saved the day.

"You might not be a hunter," CPO Jeffery said, giving me a rubdown, "but you sure are expert at knowing when danger lurks in the water."

*　　*　　*

It turned out I was an expert at sensing danger from the sky, too. The Japanese had become more and more aggressive. They had already taken over Manchuria and Korea, and now they set their sights on China. They wanted to control China's natural riches, like oil, and they were willing to fight anyone to get them—including us.

One day we were docked alongside the HMS *Bee*, another British Navy ship, when a very important human came on board. I could tell by the way the seamen had scrubbed everything in sight that something big was going to happen, and then we all stood on deck as a man in a fancy uniform with lots of ribbons walked up the gangplank. We were being inspected.

He stopped in front of a lot of my men and made comments that I could tell they didn't like. He barely looked at me, even though I was sitting at attention and giving him my best smile.

He was putting the sailors through drills when I sensed something bad was coming. A buzzing sound. A new one.

Danger! I barked. *Danger in the sky!*

The fancy admiral glared at me, and the skipper tried to get me to be quiet.

I can't be quiet. Danger is coming, I barked.

And I didn't stop. If anything, I got louder. Then I pointed in the direction of the sound.

As I've said, humans' ears are practically useless. They looked where I was pointing and finally saw the black speck in the distance. It was a Japanese warplane, and as it came near, the plane swooped much too low, right over the *Gnat* and the *Bee*, before rising again and disappearing into the distance. It was sending us a message, trying to scare us. But we didn't scare that easy.

The admiral watched it go and then finally showed me some respect. "Remarkable," he said, looking at me. "The time is coming, I fear, when we all may need a dog like this stationed on the ship's bridge."

It's about time you noticed!

Even though I had proved myself an expert at sensing danger on the river and in the skies, those silly seamen were still surprised when I proved I could protect them on land, too.

We were docked in Hankow, where our orders were to fly the flag and protect the city. It was a fun assignment. There was lots of entertainment—not to mention ice cream—in the city. I joined a sailors' club, the Strong Toppers' Club, with my men. It was a place where we went to play games and relax. I howled along when they sang their club song:

Strong Toppers are we
On the dirty Yangtze
Gunboats or cruisers
We're here for a spree.

There was other fun to be had, too. There were games of rugby and soccer and field hockey with other ships. I was really good at scoring goals, even if I did sometimes score for the other team.

But my favorite thing in Hankow was the long runs I took with my seamen, especially CPO Jeffery and Vic

Oliver, who had saved me from drowning. It was on one of those runs that I proved I could take care of my guys no matter what.

Jeffery and I were out for a walk on a Hankow road. We soon left the city behind. The dense jungle that stretched along the Yangtze was on our left, and I could smell the river a short distance away. And then I smelled something else.

Danger!

An animal was stalking us—stalking Jeffery. It wasn't a deer. We had already spotted one of those and it was harmless. This was a new smell. It was musky and big and I smelled hunger behind it. Something hungry had its eyes on my man.

I left Jeffery and darted into the jungle to scare it away, but stopped short when I found it.

Uh-oh. This thing isn't going to be afraid of me.

This new thing was some kind of big cat and it was covered in spots. It opened its mouth wide and hissed in warning when it saw me, and I saw lots of sharp teeth. But I guess it didn't want trouble. It turned its back on me and took two slow steps deeper into the forest. Then it looked at me over its shoulder through narrowed eyes.

I yelped with fear and relief as it padded away.

Jeffery called to me and I burst out of the jungle, trembling all over. He tried to get me to slow down and walk by his side, but I darted toward Hankow, forcing him to run to keep up. I knew he had to run or that big cat could come after us again.

He got the message and hurried after me.

After a while we turned and I saw it again, lurking on the side of the road, half-hidden by the jungle. Jeffery saw it, too, and we picked up our pace. It wasn't until we got back to town that I learned the cat's name.

"Judy saved me from a forest leopard today," Jeffery told everyone. "She risked her life to save mine."

Of course I did, I thought. *That's my job.*

CHAPTER 3

PUPPY LOVE

By July 1937, the Japanese stopped simply *acting* aggressive and started bombing Chinese cities. It began with a small battle, which they used as an excuse to drop their bombs and bring lots of troops into China.

In August, the Imperial Japanese Army set its sights on Shanghai. One million Japanese soldiers, backed by Japan's navy and air force, were on the outskirts of the city. Planes dropped bombs on the Chinese, and they were forced to abandon Shanghai.

On the Yangtze we were untouched—at least for now—but it was hard to see our Chinese friends suffer. Our job hadn't changed. It wasn't England's war to fight. So we continued patrolling the river to protect English merchant ships and English citizens in China.

We teamed up with an American gunboat, the USS *Panay*, and stuck to the river's main channel between Shanghai and Hankow. We avoided the places farther inland with their steep gorges and wild, unprotected lands, not to mention pirates.

I liked the Americans and they liked me. One night we were all out in one of the small riverside villages when the Americans decided they liked me so much they wanted to keep me. At the end of the night, they brought me back to their ship. I could hear poor Tankey stumbling around the riverbank, calling my name. I barked to let him know where I was.

I'm here, Tankey. With the Americans.

Those silly human ears of his didn't hear me.

Tankey didn't know where I was until the next day. A villager who did some work on the *Panay* saw me and let him know. Tankey demanded my return.

"We don't have your dog," the Americans lied. "She must still be in the village."

I don't think the Americans would have kept me forever, but their trick was going on too long. I had a good time at first, and they fed me some pretty good chow, but I was tired of being hidden away belowdecks. And I missed my men.

That night, I heard quiet, sneaky noises. But they weren't pirate noises. I suspected it was Tankey, so I didn't bark. I smelled him first and then heard him slip aboard like a pirate.

I'm here, friend. Come and find me.

But instead of searching for me, Tankey stayed on deck.

I hope you're playing a trick to get me back, I thought.

The next morning, the Americans got out of bed to discover that their ship's bell was stolen in the night.

Gotcha!

After much conversation and worry that they would get into trouble with their skipper, the Americans sent a signal to the *Gnat*: "Boarded in the night by pirates. Ship's bell stolen."

The *Gnat* replied, "We were also pirated—of Judy. Will swap one bell belonging to USS *Panay* for one lady named

Judy, property of officers and ship's company of HMS *Gnat*."

The exchange was made a few minutes later. The Americans walked me down the gangway and we met Tankey and the bell on the dock. I jumped on Tankey and gave him a good lick. You can't blame the Americans for wanting me. But I was loyal to my men and they were loyal to me.

I hoped the two ships would have many years of fun together, but the Japanese, with much of China now under their power, soon turned their aggression on us.

In December 1937, the USS *Panay* left us to sail to Nanking to evacuate the Americans still in the war-torn capital city. The gunboat was carrying members of the American embassy and escorting American cargo ships down the Yangtze. Suddenly, bombs starting falling all around them. Three oil-carrying ships were hit and set on fire. And the *Panay*, the ship where I had had such a jolly time during my "dognapping," sank to the bottom of the river. Most of the people on board made it to safety on the lifeboats, but the *Panay* would never sail again.

On the same day, Japanese airplanes zoomed out of nowhere to drop their bombs on our sister ship, HMS *Ladybird*, and the British steamships she was protecting. Then they let loose with big guns hidden on the riverbank. The *Bee* raced to her rescue, but the *Ladybird* had been hit repeatedly. Some of my friends were killed. Many more were injured.

Everyone was shocked and angry. The American and British governments protested, but the Japanese said the attacks on our ships were an accident. They claimed they had mistaken our ships—with their big American and British flags painted on their sides—for Chinese gunboats.

That's a big fat lie! I thought angrily.

In the end, Japan accepted responsibility and repaid the governments for the ships, but life became a lot more difficult for the western ships and the western people in China.

Still, it was worse for our Chinese friends. Nanking fell to Japan on December 13. We heard terrible reports about what was happening to the people left behind, but we were powerless to help.

The next year, 1938, was full of small clashes with the Japanese. We made sure to fly our British flag, but we were always ready to open up our antiaircraft guns if we had to. It wasn't unusual for Japanese officers to board the *Gnat* and other western ships, looking for Chinese who might be in hiding, or because they believed they had been insulted in some way. I had never forgotten that it was Japanese sailors who had gone after me when I was a puppy in Mr. Soo's shop, and I could tell by the way they looked at me now that most of them would have done the same thing.

Just try it, I snarled. *I'm a lot bigger than I was then, and so are my teeth.*

It wasn't long before Tankey and Jeffery started confining me belowdecks whenever the Japanese came on board.

I thought the Japanese were my biggest problem, but then I learned I would have to say goodbye to my best friends. My favorite humans had to leave the *Gnat* for new ships, including Tankey, Jeffery, and Oliver, the man who had saved me from the river when I fell overboard.

Each of them gave me a good pet before they left, and I licked their hands one last time. It was sad, and I knew I would miss them. But I was the ship's dog, so I had to stay with the ship.

I'll take care of the Gnat, I told them. *Those new humans are going to need me to show them the ropes.*

And they did.

Two of the new men who came on board—Seaman Law and Seaman "Bonny" Boniface—showed some promise as best friends, so I spent most of my time with them. They were the ones who noticed when I fell in love.

French and American gunboats, the *Francis Garnier* and the USS *Tutuila*, had docked opposite us in Hankow. Even though there was still tension with the Japanese, the sailors had a good time together. There were parties and rifle matches and a lot of teasing. There was also a very handsome English pointer on the *Francis Garnier* named Paul. Paul was so handsome, in fact, that he looked almost exactly like me, just bigger.

Paul took one look at me and fell in love. Who can blame him? But I played hard to get. He spent a lot of time showing off to get my attention whenever I was on deck or on the riverbank, running from one end of his ship to another at top speed. He was running so fast one day that he flew right off the bow and into the harbor!

Help! I barked. *Dog overboard!*

I ran down the gangway with Bonny right behind me.

The harbor wasn't anywhere near as rough as the choppy waves I had fallen into, and Paul was a strong swimmer. He swam right toward me, and Bonny pulled him from the water.

I felt sorry for Paul and licked his face to make sure he was okay. And that's when I fell in love. Even the humans could see we were made for each other.

That afternoon, Bonny and a few of the other sailors sat me down for a talk.

"We've decided you can get engaged today, and if all goes well, you'll be married tomorrow," Bonny said. "But only on one condition—that you name your first pup Bonny."

I agreed, of course, and Bonny slipped a silver anklet over my left paw.

"That is your engagement ring," he said.

The next day, Bonny and one of the French sailors married us. All of the humans cheered and clapped.

"I am pleased to pronounce you . . ." Bonny stopped and looked around. "What should I call them?" he asked.

A Frenchman yelled, "One! Call them one."

"I am pleased to pronounce you one," Bonny said.

And that's how I became a married lady. Paul and I had a three-day honeymoon on the *Gnat*, and then Paul was led back to the *Francis Garnier*. He protested, but I understood. We were ships' dogs and had to stay with our ships. He would have company soon enough—our puppies! I was happy to become a mother, but I was scared for my pups because they were born during a war.

Japanese warplanes flew overhead to bomb Chinese cities nearly every day. The Japanese kept their promise to leave the western gunboats alone, but I snarled at the sky every time the warplanes went by.

Planes thundered across the sky the very day my puppies were born. Ten beautiful English pointer puppies. Only this time, the Japanese dropped their bombs in the river all around us.

Help! I barked, circling my body around my brand-new puppies. *Help!*

It was as if the Chinese heard me. There was a different buzzing sound, and Chinese fighter planes chased the Japanese away. We were safe—for now. Once again the Japanese claimed it was an accident.

Another lie, I thought.

My puppies grew strong in spite of the Japanese. Everyone from the surrounding ships came to admire them. It wasn't long before they were exploring every corner of the *Gnat* on their chubby little legs, just as I had explored Shanghai. Watching them made everyone happy, something we all needed more of with war waging all around us.

Too soon, my puppies were big enough to leave me. One dog was a fine mascot for a gunship, but eleven were too many. I knew my puppies would have to join ships of their own, so when the *Francis Garnier* came back to Hankow from operations downriver, I was happy to see two of my pups go to live with their father. Others went to protect the British consulate in Hankow and to

American ships. I was sad for a while, but I knew they were doing important work.

Monsoon season—a time of great winds and heavy rains—was nearly upon us when the Japanese overran Hankow in October 1938. The sailors did their best to keep me away from the Japanese troops, but I kept up my personal war against them. One day I was out for a run along the river with Bonny and Seaman Law when I stopped to snarl at a Japanese sentry.

He screamed and raised his foot to give me a kick, but I danced out of his way. Then I rose up on my hind legs and growled at him.

I'm not afraid of you, kicker!

He grabbed his rifle and leveled it at my head.

Okay, I thought. *Maybe I'm a little afraid.*

Before I even had a chance to run, Seaman Law grabbed the sentry in a big bear hug and threw him into the river!

Take that, you kicker!

The sentry rose up sputtering, and we ran for the *Gnat*. We all had a good laugh about it later, but our skipper didn't think it was as funny as we did. For the next few days, I had to hide out while Japanese diplomats and officers came aboard. It took a lot of meetings, but they finally decided that they wouldn't go after Bonny and Law as long as I stayed on the ship and didn't bother the Japanese troops—at least when we were in Hankow.

It's okay, I told Bonny. *It's worth being cooped up, just to see that Japanese sentry get thrown in the river!*

We did our best to do our job and patrol the river over the next month, but seeing the devastation around us caused by the war was tough. More and more of the country was bombed into surrender by the Japanese.

It wasn't long before the British government decided they needed newer, bigger, more powerful ships on the Yangtze in case they had to fight the Japanese. I would have to say goodbye to the *Gnat* and become the mascot of a new gunboat, the HMS *Grasshopper*.

CHAPTER 4

THE *GRASSHOPPER*

In June 1939, most of the *Gnat*'s crew, including me, were transferred to the HMS *Grasshopper*.

The *Grasshopper* was a good ship, newer and shinier than the *Gnat*, but I missed all my comfortable old nooks and crannies. Even worse, Law and Bonny, my two best friends, stayed behind as part of a small crew on the *Gnat*. I had always been good at finding new humans when I needed to, but I was sick of all the constant changes.

Will I ever be as happy here as I was on my old ship? I wondered.

I had just started to get used to my new ship when Adolf Hitler, the German chancellor, invaded Poland, which led England and France to declare war on Germany. It was only a matter of time before Japan and Germany teamed up, so we were given orders to sail to England's stronghold in the Pacific—Singapore—with a stop in Hong Kong along the way.

The *Grasshopper* and two other new gunboats, the HMS *Scorpion* and the HMS *Dragonfly*, headed to open seas. Before this, I had spent most of my life on the river. As choppy and rough as those waters could be, they were nothing compared with the wild waves on the South China Sea.

I spent the first leg of the trip losing my lunch. Seasickness is no joke, and when you're a ship's dog, it's especially embarrassing. The crew tried to force me to eat and drink and exercise.

Just leave me alone, I whimpered. *I'm not getting out of bed.*

But they wouldn't leave me alone. Eating was out of the question, but they were able to get me to drink and walk on the deck. Slowly I began to get my sea legs, and soon I was able to eat. I never got seasick again.

Even though war raged in Europe and in China, you'd

hardly know it in Singapore. There was an active naval presence, but there was also lots of fun to be had. Until I found my own private war.

It happened—as bad things seem to—when I was off the ship. I went on a visit to the family of a local official with three children who loved dogs. Have I mentioned how awesome kids are to play with? But while I was away, my sailors got into trouble in the form of a monkey named Mickey.

While I was off playing, the *Grasshopper*'s new crew agreed to keep the monkey on board while his ship was on duty somewhere in the Pacific. The minute I got home, I realized why Mickey's men didn't want him around when they were on duty. He was a menace.

Mickey took one look at me and jumped on my back.

I'm not a horse! I barked.

I jumped and bucked and leaped, but that stupid monkey didn't let go. I had no choice but to demand help. I sat down and howled until the monkey jumped off my back and threw an arm around my neck.

The sailors, instead of helping me, thought it was hilarious.

Stop laughing, I howled at the crew. *It's not funny!*

Thankfully, I figured out pretty quickly that the annoying ball of fur was attached to a sort of metal leash, so I simply ran out of its range.

I did my best to avoid the screeching thing for the next few days, staying far enough away that he couldn't dive onto my back again. And okay, I'll admit it—I may have used that distance to drive Mickey a little crazy. That's what I was doing when George White came on board.

Coxswain White joined the *Grasshopper* at Keppel Harbor in Singapore. He marched up the gangway to report for duty, only to have Mickey the monkey dive-bomb his head. Mickey snatched White's sailor's cap and jumped up and down, taunting him.

Sailors nearby burst into laughter.

Let's see how you handle this, sailor.

White was up to the test. He grabbed Mickey, snatched his cap back, and tossed that cheeky monkey onto the deck.

That's when White spotted me. "You're laughing your head off, aren't you?" he asked me.

I am, I barked.

From then on, White was one of my special humans.

I had a new ship, a new special human, and Mickey would soon be put off the *Grasshopper* forever. Life in Singapore was going to be good—if only the war would stay far away.

And for eighteen months it did. We shuttled between Singapore and Hong Kong, but tensions between England and the Japanese Empire continued to grow. Japan wanted the food, minerals, and oil in Singapore, Malaysia, and the Dutch East Indies, and was willing to go to war with any country standing in her way. That included England and the United States.

At 0400 hours on December 8, 1941, World War II officially came to the Pacific. It was still December 7 across the international date line in Hawaii when Japanese warplanes dropped bombs on the United States naval base in Pearl Harbor. At the same time, bombs rained down on Singapore, the Philippines, and other islands in

Southeast Asia. Japan also landed troops in Malaysia to try to push into Singapore by land. The attacks were a complete surprise.

I barked and barked as the planes approached, and my guys ran for the antiaircraft guns, but gunboats didn't have the speed or the gun power to put up much of a fight. We weighed anchor and pulled out to sea. England's real battleships, the HMS *Prince of Wales* and HMS *Repulse*, set sail from Jamaica to come and help, but two days later a Japanese submarine spotted them. Bombs soon rained down on them from the skies while torpedoes hit them from under the sea. In just two hours, England lost any ability to stop the Japanese in the Pacific. America's fleet was also destroyed in the first round of attacks.

We were at war, but how would we fight back?

Our land forces were being overrun, and the *Grasshopper*, along with the *Dragonfly* and the *Scorpion*, spent days zigzagging across the sea or creeping along the coast, hoping our small size would make us hard to see and easy for Japanese bombers to ignore. We moved freely only at night, searching for enemy targets to attack or

British troops to rescue. My dog ears became more and more important, letting the gunships know when warplanes were near.

One night, British soldiers who were battling the Japanese on land got cut off from the rest of the troops. There were 1,500 men stuck in the jungle who needed to be rescued. Creeping through the jungle at night in search of them, I knew not to bark. I did nudge our leader's arm when I sensed the Japanese were near, and we all stopped until the danger passed. I didn't even scratch my neck, knowing that my jingling collar could give us away. We found the troops and led them out of the jungle and onto the gunships right under the Japanese soldiers' noses!

Take that, you kickers!

Another time, though, on a similar rescue by the *Grasshopper* and the *Dragonfly*, we ran into trouble. We had found our soldiers and were nearly back to the ships when the Japanese spotted us. There was a short battle while we got the British soldiers on board, but a sailor from the *Dragonfly* named Les Searle was shot in the leg. He made it back to the ship and later to the hospital in Singapore.

I visited him, and all the other wounded soldiers, whenever our ship's medic made the trip.

Get well soon, friends, I thought.

Keeping the troops' spirits up became a more important part of my job, especially as the war news got worse. By the end of January, most of the area was in Japanese hands. Singapore, Britain's stronghold, was under siege and on the verge of collapse. Everywhere I looked, there was rubble. Refugees streamed toward the harbor, hoping to find a way off the island before the Japanese arrived.

By early February 1942, the first Japanese troops entered Singapore. We were forced to evacuate the island, and the only escape was by sea. Everyone in the city— soldiers, government workers, the English, and the Chinese families who worked for them—was faced with finding a place on a ship or being made prisoner of the Japanese. Bombs fell while people crowded the pier to fight for a spot on anything that would float, from the smallest fishing boats to yachts and gunboats.

On February 13, the *Grasshopper* became home to a lot of frightened mothers and children. Each person was met with a cup of tea and a piece of chocolate by my good friend George White. My job was to wag my tail, lick little fingers, and bark hello.

Welcome to the Grasshopper, I told them. *You're safe here.*

It was after midnight before we were finally able to leave the harbor. I found a spot between two of the children and kept them calm until they were able to fall asleep. I tried to sleep myself, but my ears were listening for the sounds of Japanese warplanes so I could warn my sailors if they came near.

The *Grasshopper* and the *Dragonfly* planned to sail at night and anchor near one of the hundreds of small volcanic islands during the day. With luck, we'd make it to Java and larger ships that could take us safely to India or Australia—far away from the Japanese war machine.

But as I've already warned you, luck wasn't on our side.

CHAPTER 5

TRAPPED

Dawn broke and we were nowhere near land. It was just after nine o'clock when I heard it—a plane coming toward us.

Danger! I barked, pointing in the direction of the noise. *Danger!*

A Japanese flying boat, or seaplane, was suddenly overhead. It dropped a bomb over the *Grasshopper*, but luckily, it missed. The children hid their heads and screamed, and I watched as the seaplane turned to head for the *Dragonfly*. It dropped a bomb that landed close enough to cause damage.

The seaplane disappeared as quickly as it had arrived,

but its primary job wasn't to drop bombs. It was a search plane. We knew our position had been radioed to other Japanese forces, which meant enemy ships and planes were already on their way.

We headed for the Lingga Archipelago, a small island chain where we hoped to hide from incoming bombers. We were within two miles of land when the warplanes arrived—more than a hundred of them.

I barked and barked—*Get away from us. We have children on this ship*—but there was little we could do. The attacks came every five minutes, wave after wave of bombings. Somehow we managed to avoid them all.

The captain of the *Dragonfly* knew we had women and children on board, so he steered the ship away from us, hoping to bring the Japanese with him.

Meanwhile, the *Grasshopper* zigzagged through the water for nearly two hours, trying to avoid the relentless bombings. We managed to escape attack after attack, but we were still a half mile from land when a bomb hit. I had just gone belowdecks to check on my men there when it happened.

Boom!

The bomb hit the part of the ship where most of the women and children were staying. I had been with them just seconds before.

The skipper managed to get the *Grasshopper* close to shore. Lifeboats were lowered, and my men helped the civilians who were still alive board them. Once the civilians were off the ship, the order came that no captain ever wants to give:

"Abandon ship! Abandon ship!"

Sailors jumped into the waist-high water and tried to make their way to shore. I should have been with them. I wanted to be with them. But I was trapped beneath a pile of metal lockers that had fallen over on top of me. I had just enough room to stand, but I couldn't move backward or forward, and there wasn't enough room to turn around. I tried to push the lockers aside, but they were too heavy. Water rushed in. I remembered when I had fallen into the Yangtze and struggled to keep my head above water.

You didn't drown then, I told myself. *You won't now, either.*

Two more bombs fell nearby but didn't hit the ship. The water level settled around me. It came up to my neck but didn't cover my face. I could breathe. The planes started firing their machine guns, and I howled, hoping someone would hear me.

No one did.

I was trapped and alone.

I have to get to my people, I thought. *They need me.*

I waited and waited. Hours went by, and then I heard something. A human was walking around the wreckage. I sniffed, trying to place who it was, but all I could smell was burning oil and gasoline.

Is it a Japanese kicker? I wondered. *Or is it one of my guys?*

The noise got louder.

I whimpered, quietly. If it was a kicker, I wasn't sure I wanted to be found.

The footsteps got closer, and I whimpered again.

And then there were hands reaching for me and shoving the lockers aside. It was my friend George White, the man who had conquered Mickey the monkey. White had found me!

As soon as I could, I shook myself dry and licked his face. He was safe, and he had found me!

We went up on deck and White shouted to the people on the beach. "Hey, I found Judy! She's alive!"

There was a cheer, and I barked at them to let them know I was okay. Then White and I gathered up all the food we could find. He made a raft from loose timber and we rowed toward shore.

I joined the survivors of the *Grasshopper*. There weren't nearly enough of them. Most were hidden at the edge of the jungle on what was a small, uninhabited island. The first thing I smelled was fear. I also smelled hunger and thirst mixed with worry.

"Did anyone find fresh water yet?" White asked the captain.

The captain shook his head. "No water anywhere," he said. He eyed the survivors. "We won't last long without it."

I patrolled the beach, keeping an eye out for the Japanese. That's when I smelled it—water! I pawed through the sand.

A British Royal Marine who had come on board in Singapore noticed. "Hey, Chief, I think your dog's found a bone or something," he told White.

I didn't have time to correct him. If he had a dog's nose, he'd know. I had found an underground spring.

White came over to check out what I was doing. At that very moment, water bubbled up out of the wet sand. He put his fingers in the stream and licked them.

"Water!" he yelled. "Judy's found us fresh water!"

He helped me dig, and soon there was a small fountain of water. White and the men caught as much as they could in pots, and everybody—including me—had a good drink. We made hot cocoa and rice for dinner.

One of the survivors raised his cup and toasted me.

"To Judy!"

Everyone else did the same, and there was a chorus of "To Judy! To Judy!"

I raised my head and wagged my tail, happy to have been able to help. Then I snuggled down between two of the civilian survivors—the two who I could sense were the most frightened and needed me the most.

A couple of hours later, a small whaler boat ran ashore on our beach. I bounded over when I realized who had come to talk to our captain. It was Les Searle, the *Dragonfly* sailor I had visited in the hospital. He was as happy to see me as I was to see him.

He told us the story of what had happened to our sister ship after she tried to draw the Japanese away from us.

The *Dragonfly* had taken a direct bomb hit, and then two more. Explosions ripped the boat apart while sailors desperately tried to launch a lifeboat and rubber life rafts. It took only minutes for the *Dragonfly* to sink beneath the sea.

The water was filled with men, clinging to rafts or bits of the wreckage. The planes returned to shoot at them with machine guns. Bullets ripped across the surface of the water while men dove below to try to stay alive.

The survivors made their way to an atoll, a small island formed from coral, not too far from the island we had washed up on. They didn't have super senses like mine to find water, so they were in serious trouble. They also had a number of wounded men and no medical supplies. Searle and White set out to collect the *Dragonfly* survivors and bring them to us.

The fire on the *Grasshopper* was still burning when White and Searle came back with the survivors the next morning. Ammunition left on our ship led to one small explosion after another. The sounds mixed with the moans of the wounded, and then there was one final explosion that took the whole ship.

I stood next to White and watched the *Grasshopper* go up in flames. If he hadn't found me, I would have died in that explosion.

I licked his hand. *Thank you, friend. You saved my life.*

Over the next few days, more survivors from other islands found us, and they brought news. The nearby island of Singkep held a Dutch colonial government office, and there were rumors of a rescue operation there. One of my men set sail on a small fishing craft for Singkep to find out if it was true.

While we waited, I did my best to make sure all my humans were doing okay. We survived on coconuts and the water I had discovered. I also killed lots of snakes, but no one was desperate enough to eat them—at least not yet.

Finally, five days after we abandoned ship, we spotted a tongkang, a small wooden cargo boat, heading toward our beach. The Dutch on Singkep had sent it to us so the survivors could be ferried off our desert island. I don't know how many trips it took to transport us all, but I stood guard and made sure I was one of the last to leave.

On Singkep we were given food, water, a tongkang, and instructions. "Make your way to Sumatra," the Dutch official told us, "and then find a seaworthy ship that's big enough to get you to India or Australia. Whatever you do, stay out of Japanese hands."

We followed his advice and hoped we were headed for safety.

CHAPTER 6

A DANGEROUS
JOURNEY

Sumatra, the sixth-largest island in the world, sits on the equator. It's a land of wild jungles, raging rivers, and steep mountains. From the island's east coast, we had to travel across the entire island—about three hundred miles—to the west coast and a ship to freedom. For now, the Dutch still held the island, but it was only a matter of time before it fell to the Japanese.

One of my favorite humans, George White, didn't sail with us. He and two other men decided to take their chances on whatever small boat they could find and sail the 2,680 miles to India across the open sea. My job, as always, was to stay with my ship's crew and keep them safe. I gave George's hand a final goodbye lick and climbed the tongkang's gangway.

When I got on board, I curled up next to Les Searle and hoped for the best.

We reached the coast of Sumatra and the mouth of the powerful Indragiri River two days later. The tongkang pushed as far inland as it could before sailing became impossible. Huge animals I had never seen before roamed the thick jungle on either side of us and lounged on the riverbanks—Sumatran tigers, crocodiles, elephants, leopards, rhinos, apes, and more. The snakes—vipers, cobras, and kraits—were familiar from my time on the desert island. The mosquitoes, fire ants, leeches, scorpions, and other crawling things were ones we already knew too well.

We had to trek through the dense rain forest and the mountains by foot to a railroad. From there, we would catch a train to the port city of Padang.

I took the lead on our trek, looking for solid ground and alerting my humans to any threats that stood in our way. One of those threats included a crocodile that didn't slip back into the river when we neared. I growled at it, warning it to get away, but I accidentally got a little too close.

Ouch!

I danced back just in time to escape its giant jaws, but it managed to slash my shoulder with its claws before it escaped into the river. From then on, I was careful to keep my distance while I barked warnings at the beasts, but there was no way I was going to let a crocodile ambush my humans. Once I even had to scare away a hungry tiger!

For most of our trek, we had to walk single file under relentless rain, carrying the wounded on stretchers made of tree branches. We ate what we could find, and I supplied what I could catch. Mostly snakes and flying foxes.

It took three weeks, but we finally made our way to Sawah Luento and its train station on March 15. Rumor had it that the Japanese army was rapidly advancing, so we lost no time hopping a train for the final fifty miles to Padang and freedom.

There were cries of "There's the sea!" as the train

reached the top of a hill over Padang on the morning of March 16. But an old man met us at the station with terrible news. "The last ship left—you just missed it."

A minute before, I could smell hope, and now I smelled only despair. I padded from human to human, trying to raise their spirits, but it was nearly impossible.

The Dutch still controlled the city, but just barely. Surrender to the Japanese had already been arranged. We spent the night on the docks, hoping that the Dutch were wrong and another boat would come to our rescue. None did. The next day, the men were ordered to give up any weapons they had and take shelter in a school to wait for the Japanese.

I heard them and smelled them before the others. Motorcycles and trucks outside, and then boots pounding through the school. Searle made a leash from the cloth of his torn pants and slipped it around my collar.

Japanese soldiers marched in, shouting words no one understood with swords jangling at their sides. One of them pointed at me, yelled something, and swept out of the room. The others followed him.

A low growl rose in my throat—*kickers*—but Searle shushed me.

Are they going to kill us all? I wondered.

But they had other plans for us.

On March 17, 1942, the Japanese made us prisoners of war. We wouldn't be executed—for now.

The next day, the Japanese separated the men and me from the women and children, and sent them to a different camp. Then the men were marched to the Dutch army barracks. I joined the British, Australian, and Dutch sailors, soldiers, and airmen as we trudged across town. Japanese guards rushed us along, prodding the men with their rifles. My men were exhausted, dirty, hungry, embarrassed, and defeated.

I raised my head and wagged my tail, marching alongside them. *Let's show them we're not broken*, I wanted to say. Slowly the men around me understood. Heads rose, spines straightened, and steps quickened. Even the wounded showed their pride.

We would need that strength and pride to survive. It

was a struggle just to stay alive on the food rations provided by the Japanese. Searle had done his best to show the enemy that I was a full member of the Royal Navy, but there were no rations for me. I was hungry all the time. It was the same desperate hunger I had felt in my early days alone in Shanghai. Searle and his buddies gave me what they could spare, but even they sometimes scrounged through our guards' trash, searching for something to eat.

So I learned to hunt for my own food. Lizards, snakes, rats, and whatever rice the men could spare made up my diet. I shared what I caught with my men. Still, we never had enough.

The days were filled with boredom and hunger. Hunger and boredom. Weeks went by and word came that we were being moved to Belawan, a port city in Sumatra. A long caravan of trucks arrived. I wasn't welcome by the Japanese, so Searle and his buddies had to sneak me on board and hide me under some rice sacks for the hot, five-day journey across the island.

When we reached Belawan, I smelled fear. No one had

told the men what would happen next. Would we sail for Japan?

I had worries of my own. *Will Searle be able to sneak me on board a ship? Or will I be left behind to fend for myself?*

Shortly after we arrived in Belawan, our Japanese colonel stood on a box and spoke to the men for the first time.

"I am your father and you are my children," Colonel Banno said. "You must obey me or I will cut off your heads."

He waited a moment to let that sink in.

"I hope you will be happy in my camp. My fondest hope is that you will all go home after Japan has won the war."

He didn't tell the men where that camp was or what would happen to them when they got there.

I hid out as best I could around the docks while the men waited in dark, one-room huts to discover their fate. It didn't take long. Instead of boarding a ship, they were forced into railcars with no windows, light, or air. Once again I slipped in unnoticed with Searle and his buddies.

Luckily, the trip was short. On June 27, 1942, we entered a camp in Gloegoer, a suburb of the Sumatran city of Medan. We found ourselves crowded into what had been Dutch army barracks—even more crowded than those in Padang.

Rations were less than they had been—a cup of watery rice in the morning and some kind of boiled flour for dinner. The men had nothing to spare for me, so once again I took up hunting.

The guards were angry and mean. They kicked and threw stones when they saw me. I hated them, and they knew it. But I was still faster than their boots.

After many days locked up in the barracks, the men were finally allowed outside and put to work. Some worked on building an airfield so Japanese planes could land. Others cleared the jungle to build a Japanese temple. Work was often accompanied by brutal beatings if the men didn't move fast enough.

I made new friends while I was slinking around camp and traveling to the work sites to protect my men from snakes. One of my new friends, "Cobbler" Cousens, was a man who made and repaired boots for the Japanese soldiers. He used to slip me small pieces of leather. They were hard to chew and even harder to digest, but at least it was something.

Months passed, and with each one it seemed our food rations got smaller and smaller. The men were desperate, and sometimes that meant they did foolish things.

One day Cousens talked Searle into helping him steal a sack of rice that was unguarded. They hid it under a blanket in the back of the barracks.

The next day, two guards marched into the barracks, shouting and demanding to inspect everything. The men got more and more desperate as the guards moved through the barracks. My friends Cousens and Searle were especially scared. If the Japanese discovered that rice, they would be beaten to death.

I have to do something!

We had all noticed that the Japanese were terrified of death—human skeletons and graves especially made them jumpy. I dashed to a graveyard where the local Sumatrans buried their dead and looked for an old grave. I silently apologized to the skeleton I uncovered, and then I raced back to the barracks.

You should have seen the kickers' faces when I ran in with a human skull between my teeth!

They screamed and yelled while I made three loops around the room. Then, just as they were about to raise their rifles, I dropped the skull and dashed out of the room. The guards scurried out behind me, too afraid to finish their inspection.

Ha!

Not only did I scare the guards, my men got to keep their rice and their lives.

Sadly, the extra rice didn't come in time to help my cobbler friend Cousens. Soon after that, he got sick and was carried to the hospital hut. I knew that men who went in there hardly ever came out alive. I waited and waited, but my friend was gone. Searle did his best to cheer me up, but I was very sad.

I miss my friend.

I didn't know it then, but I was about to make a new friend—one who would turn out to be my best friend for the rest of my life.

CHAPTER 7

FRANK AND ME

After my friend Cousens died, I spent more and more time nosing around the camp for food. The men were starving and mostly couldn't share. Then one day, in August 1942, I passed a man in the eating area. I had seen him around, but we hadn't really met yet. Frank Williams had the same tiny bit of rice that the rest of the men had, but he could see I was hungry.

He poured some of the watery rice into his palm.

"Come on, Judy," he said. "This is yours."

I whined. I knew Frank was starving. I gave him a chance to change his mind.

He didn't. Instead, he set his whole plate on the ground and petted me while I slurped it up.

I settled in next to him. Underneath Frank's dirt and sweat I could smell kindness, and something else—a sense of adventure. I learned later that before he joined the RAF (Royal Air Force), Frank had been a merchant marine, sailing on ships that carried goods to ports around the world. Frank and I had both gone to sea in search of friendship and adventure. Maybe that's why we became such good friends.

It wasn't long before I knew I was meant to be Frank's dog, and he was meant to be my human. He knew it, too. From then on we were inseparable. And we kept each other alive.

One of our first adventures together involved coming up with a great plan for stealing food from the temple grounds, where the Japanese guards left fruit at the shrine. While Frank worked, I hid in a bush and listened for his whistle. When the coast was clear, I dashed to the shrine, grabbed the fruit, and ran back into the bush. At the end of Frank's workday, we shared our feast hidden in the jungle.

Frank taught me lots of things. I knew that when he snapped his fingers a certain way, I had to hide from the guards and not come back until he snapped again. We also did tricks for the other POWs to keep their spirits up. I could do all the usual things like sit and roll over, but Frank also taught me how to hide on command. I'd slip under his bunk and then reappear at the other end of the barracks before anyone even knew I was gone. The men loved it.

I continued to hunt at night, and I brought Frank everything I caught and killed so we could share. On one of my nighttime treks into the jungle, I met a nice dog and we spent some time together. And boy was Frank surprised when he discovered I was going to have more puppies! On November 18, 1942, they were born—five of them. I didn't know it then, but Frank and one of my puppies would save my life and help me make military history.

Colonel Banno, like the other Japanese soldiers in camp, didn't like dogs. As rations got smaller and smaller—even for them—I began to think they were looking at me like I was their next dinner. But he had a local lady friend who loved me. Whenever she came to camp, she called me to her. As long as Banno wasn't standing right next to her, I was happy to visit because she always slipped me a treat.

One day Frank figured out that Banno would be leaving camp to visit his girlfriend, and that's when he came up with his plan. He hid in the bushes with one of my pups—Kish, the cutest one—and carried him into Banno's quarters. That alone was enough to get Frank shot, but when Kish waddled across the colonel's desk, Banno burst out laughing. Frank used sign language to suggest that Banno give Kish to his girlfriend as a present, and Banno loved the idea.

Then Frank got to his real request. He told the colonel how important I was to morale, how much harder the men worked when I was around, and how the guards threatened to shoot me on a regular basis.

"If you make Judy a prisoner of war, she'll be protected," Frank said.

Banno said he couldn't. Japanese records were very precise. How would he explain an extra prisoner in camp?

"Add the letter 'A' to my number," Frank suggested. "Judy can be prisoner 81-A. No need for records."

Kish was not only cute, he was smart, too. At that moment he did a somersault on the colonel's desk.

Smiling, the colonel agreed. He wrote out an official order for Frank to keep in his pocket—one that named me a prisoner of war. The men in the barracks made a tag for my collar out of a piece of old tin: *81-A Gloegoer Medan*.

I was official! The guards couldn't threaten to shoot me anymore, and I'd get to stay with Frank.

I hated saying goodbye to Kish, but he was going to a good person who loved dogs. My other pups found new homes, too. A secret request for a puppy came from the women's POW camp, and a local fruit seller smuggled Sheikje to them in her basket. Rokok snuck through a drainage pipe so he could go to the Swiss consulate in Medan. Punch and Jackie stayed in camp for as long as they could, but one day they escaped into the jungle.

They had inherited my love of adventure. I hoped they'd inherited my survival skills, too.

Things went okay after that. We were starving, but we survived. Then in April 1943, Banno left and a new officer took over—Captain Nishi. He was the meanest one yet.

On his first day, Nishi had the men assemble in the yard and stand at attention—even the men who were sick. I followed orders and stood at Frank's side.

Nishi took one look at me and stormed over, slapping his cane against his boot. I was scared, but I was mad, too, and I started to growl.

Frank pulled out the paper that made me an official POW.

That made Nishi even angrier, but Banno was a colonel and he was just a captain, so he couldn't give the order to kill me—at least not yet.

He forced the men to work—taking apart an old factory—until they could hardly stand, and then prodded them to work some more. Those who couldn't were badly beaten.

Then Nishi made an announcement: "According to the Imperial High Command, all prisoners are ordered to Singapore."

There was relief and even a little hope in the air. Singapore meant civilization and maybe news about how the war was really going. It might mean letters from home, or even Red Cross packages. Best of all, it meant no more jungle.

Frank was packing his few belongings back in the barracks when Nishi stormed in. Frank snapped his fingers and I slipped under the bunk out of sight.

"Dog not go," Nishi shouted. "Dog stay." As he strode out, the men saw a smile flit across his face.

My friend slumped on his bunk, devastated. I crept out and licked his hand.

"I won't leave you behind, girl," he said, ruffling my ears.

For the next few hours, we practiced a new trick. Frank would snap his fingers, and I'd run into the rice sack at his feet. The next time he snapped, I'd run out again and dash for cover. We did that over and over and over again.

After I had that trick down, Frank practiced standing with me in the sack while it hung over his shoulder. I had to stay very still and not give myself away. It was hot and dark and uncomfortable, but if that's what it took for Frank and me to stay together, that's what I'd do.

At dawn the next day, we were called to the yard. The line of sick and wounded was as long as the men who were considered healthy—if starving could still be "healthy." Under Nishi's mean eyes, Frank tied me to a pole with a long rope.

"Now you stay right here, girl," he said.

I licked his hand. I knew what those words really meant: *Join me as soon as the coast is clear.*

Frank stood with the others, a rice sack holding a blanket at his feet. Nishi checked his bag personally, and then looked over Frank's shoulder and gave me a cruel smile.

"Move!" he shouted to the men. "March!"

The POWs hobbled toward the gates.

Frank was near the end of the line. I watched him carefully, waiting for the signal. He had just cleared the gates when he whistled. I slipped from my knot and dashed into the jungle lining the road. I stayed out of sight until Frank was at the train station, ready to board.

Frank knelt down to tie his shoe and handed the blanket in his rice sack to another man. The prisoners formed a circle around him and then Frank snapped his fingers. I was in that sack in seconds, and we stepped onto the train.

When we reached the port city, Frank gave me the signal to hide. I hid in the only place I could think of— under the train. Then, as the prisoners were lined up and marched toward the port, I followed from whatever cover I could find. When Frank's rice sack was checked, the guards found it filled with a blanket, just like in camp.

The men were lined up to board a ship when I made my next move. I slithered on my belly like a snake in the jungle, freezing and flattening whenever a guard neared. Finally, I made my way into the row of prisoners and toward my friend. Frank dumped the blanket, and once again I jumped into his sack.

I was safe, but we had to stand for hours in the hot sun while we waited for the ship's gangway to be readied. I could feel Frank's legs swaying and buckling, but the men around him helped prop him up and keep him standing.

I kept perfectly still, just like I had been trained. The hardest part was when I smelled Captain Nishi approach my friend and heard his mean voice.

Has he found us out? I wondered. It was all I could do not to growl at him and show him my teeth.

"Dog no come?" he demanded.

"Dog no come," Frank said.

Even from inside the sack, I could sense the captain's evil joy as he strode away.

We'd made it this far. Now all we had to do was survive the ship crossing and we'd be in Singapore, together.

CHAPTER 8

TORPEDOES!

Eleven hundred human POWs and one dog were forced into the dark, airless cargo holds of the *Van Waerwijck*. The Dutch steamship, which wasn't big enough for even half that many men, had been taken by the Japanese at the beginning of the war. It was barely seaworthy and there was no red cross painted on its side to indicate that it carried prisoners.

It was June 25, 1944. I had been a POW for just over two years.

Frank fought his way to a corner in the back of the hold and let me out of the sack. We found a platform near a porthole. It let in a tiny wisp of fresh air, and we slept as the ship made its way through the dark waters. By the next morning, the men were sitting in puddles of sweat and the temperature continued to rise.

It was just after midday when the torpedoes hit.

First one explosion and then another. Smoke and steam filled the cargo hold. Salt water poured through the ship's hull.

Frank was frozen. I nudged his leg. *We have to do something!*

My friend eyed the men scrambling for the ladder that would take them out of the hold. Then he turned to the porthole and wrenched it open.

"Out you go, old girl!" he yelled.

I looked out and then looked back at him. Frank wouldn't be able to fit through that hole.

Are you sure? I wanted to ask him. *You'll be alone.*

Frank nodded at me, and I did what he asked. I pulled myself halfway through the porthole. Frank gave me a push, and the rest of me followed. I dropped fifteen feet to the water below.

The sea was filled with wreckage from our ship and

others. POWs who tried to climb on lifeboats were kicked away with boots or rifle butts. Only the Japanese were allowed on board. Everyone else had to wait.

I swam from man to man, looking for Frank. Some of them needed help finding a piece of wreckage to help them stay afloat, so I let them hold on to me until we found something. When the rescue vessels finally arrived around three hours later, men tried to pull me aboard. I swam away every time.

I have to find Frank, I thought. *I won't stop until I do.*

Finally, there were no more men left in the water, and I let a boat rescue me.

There was still no sign of Frank.

I slumped in the bottom of the boat, covered in oil and muck, sadder and more frightened than I had ever been.

When we reached port, I jumped off the boat and into the crowd of prisoners. My old friend Les Searle was there, but still no Frank.

Searle had just lifted me up to put me onto the truck

that would take us to our next POW camp when we heard Nishi's angry voice.

"Halt!" he yelled. Every inch of the Japanese captain's body shook with rage.

He screamed an order and two guards grabbed me from Searle and dropped me at Nishi's feet. The captain stood above me, screaming. As soon as he finished, I was sure the soldiers would lift their rifles and fire.

Then we heard another loud voice. "Nishi!"

It was Colonel Banno!

I don't like you, I thought, *but at least you're better than the other one.*

I didn't understand all the words flying back and forth, but it was clear that Banno was angry and Nishi was in big trouble. Searle scooped me up and put me back on the truck. We could still hear Banno yelling at Nishi as the truck drove away. The colonel had saved me once again.

It was hard to feel happy with Frank still missing.

Where is my best friend? I wondered. *Did he survive, or is he lost to the sea forever?*

Searle tried to get me to go with him into his hut when we reached River Valley Road Prison in Singapore, but I couldn't. I had to do everything I could to find Frank. I went into every building and visited every corner of that camp looking for him.

He wasn't there. He wasn't anywhere.

But there were still men arriving. So I settled just inside the front gate and waited. And waited. And waited some more. Two days later, I was about to give up hope, when I saw him practically fall out of a truck and limp through the camp's front gates.

Frank!

I was so happy to see him I knocked him right off his feet. We rolled around on the ground, saying hello. My best friend and I were together again!

Having Frank back made me feel much better, but our dreams of a better life in Singapore were quickly dashed. There was no mail, no Red Cross packages, and even less food than in Gloegoer. Men ate leaves and tree bark, and I caught as many rats as I could. It was never enough.

One bright spot was the occasional piece of war news or "V for Victory" sign passed along to us by a sympathetic Chinese local. The war wasn't going as well for the Japanese as our guards claimed. The men only had to hang on, they told each other.

"The Yanks have the enemy on the run," they whispered. "The Allies will be here soon."

Rumors began to spread of a return trip to Sumatra—this one on a mission to work on a fruit plantation harvesting crops. There would be a test, the Japanese told the men, and only the fittest prisoners would go. Every man wanted to pass that test—harvesting crops meant food to eat. Nearly everyone did pass, no matter how weak with malaria, beriberi—a disease caused by a lack of vitamins—or starvation. Only those who couldn't stand up were left behind in Singapore. The fact that the test wasn't much of a test at all should have been our first clue that the rumors weren't true.

This time around, the guards weren't interested in me. Since no one said I couldn't go, I marched beside Frank on our trip through the city to the harbor. That should have been our second clue.

If we had known what we were in for, we might have hoped for another torpedo.

We were brought ashore at Sumatra in late July and began a forced march through the jungle. We crossed rickety bridges over rushing rivers, and once, Frank had to carry me through waist-high mud. The jungle cut off all sunlight and we weren't given anything to eat or drink. The men shuffled along and eventually—after seven diffi-cult miles—we saw campfires up ahead. They didn't shed enough light for us to really see what our new home was like.

It wasn't until the next morning that we learned the truth. By now the men knew there would be no crops to harvest, but they didn't know why they were really there.

"You will have the honor of building a railway line for the emperor of Japan," a Japanese lieutenant told us.

"When it is finished, you will all receive a medal from the emperor."

It was a good thing he didn't understand the words the men mumbled about the emperor and his stupid medal.

The Japanese had decided to do what the Dutch had previously realized was impossible—build a railroad to connect the east and west coasts of Sumatra. That meant laying railroad tracks through swamps, over nine-thousand-foot-high mountains, and across raging rivers, not to mention through areas of the jungle that had never been seen by humans, not even the native Sumatrans.

It wasn't long before the men started calling it the Death Railway.

CHAPTER 9

THE DEATH RAILWAY

Life along the Death Railway was worse than anything we had faced before. There was less food, more work, and many more beatings. This time, our guards were mostly Korean. They were forced to join the Japanese Imperial Army and then sent to this jungle far from the fighting. They were angry, and they took their anger out on the prisoners.

We were awoken by the musical notes of a bugle the first morning at what the guards insisted was seven a.m. It was really four thirty, but all of Japan's territories had to be on Tokyo time.

The men were forced to work twelve or fourteen or even twenty hours a day for their meager rations—a breakfast glob of a flour-like plant substance called tapioca mixed with water, a cup of rice for lunch, and a cup of rice for dinner. Sometimes there was a watery soup with leaves in it. Men who were sick received almost nothing, which meant they couldn't get better. Sick men who could sit up were given the job of catching flies, because flies spread disease. If they didn't catch enough, they'd get no food.

Being carried into the hospital hut almost always equaled death. There were a few British doctors who were also prisoners at the camp, but they had no medical supplies.

Hunger pains kept us awake at night, as did the sounds of the jungle—buzzing insects, bellowing bullfrogs, screaming monkeys, trumpeting elephants, roaring tigers, and the squeals of wild pigs captured in the tigers' jaws. Our huts were made of palm leaves and bamboo poles, and rats ran around freely. There was no place for the men to bathe and no soap to bathe with. Between the mosquitoes, the ants, the lice, and the mites, the men never stopped scratching. Neither did I.

There were many different jobs on the railway, all of them backbreaking. The guards were always yelling, "Speedo! Speedo!," forcing the men to work faster.

Whenever the POWs didn't make their quota for the day or something broke, there were horrible beatings. The guards shouted orders no one could understand and then beat the men for not understanding. Sometimes they beat the men just because they were bored and wanted something to do.

Despite the constant threat of beatings, the men did what they could to sabotage the project. Truck engines were filled with banana mush and sand was dropped into gas tanks. Railway ties and spikes were laid into earth that would soon fall away, and some of those ties were made of wood that was about to decay.

Getting caught meant death, but the rise in morale that came with a successful sabotage effort made it worth the risk.

Foraging for food in the jungle was forbidden, but the men did it anyway—it's what kept them alive. Leaves, snakes, rats, nuts, berries, and even lizards were added to the men's dinner each night.

While Frank worked, I stayed in the jungle nearby. I caught rats, snakes, and lizards to share with the men. Often, Frank had to give me the signal to disappear when guards were near. Whenever one came too close, my lip curled back in a snarl and a low growl built in my throat. I couldn't help it, no matter how many times Frank told me to be quiet. I could smell how mean the guards were, and how much they enjoyed hurting my men.

So Frank would give me the signal to disappear, and I'd wait in the jungle until he said it was safe to come out again.

Day after day was the same—hard work, hardly any food, beatings, and not enough sleep. The men wondered if anyone knew where they were or if they had been completely forgotten. No one had ever received a letter from home. Once, in Gloegoer, the men were given postcards they could write on and send home, and then the guards made a great show of burning them in a campfire while they laughed.

Does the world think we're already dead? I wondered.

Occasionally we got good news that kept the men going. Somehow the prisoners had put together a small wireless radio from stolen bits and pieces. One of the POWs kept it hidden in his hollow artificial leg, and the men listened to war news when they could.

In October 1944, we learned that the Japanese had suffered a crushing defeat at the hands of the Americans. The news was whispered from camp to camp, POW to POW.

"Hang on," the men told each other. "Just hang on for a little while longer."

Christmas came and went. The men were not allowed to sing carols, but we did get the day off and a little extra food. Then, on January 10, 1945, we got some real hope— an American bomber appeared in the sky. It had bombed Padang! The guards started carrying gas masks everywhere. They were frightened. We were hopeful, but worried at the same time.

Will the Allies get here in time to save us? Or will we die of starvation first?

Over the next few months, the work got harder and the guards got angrier.

The angrier the guards got, the angrier I became. More than once I tricked them into stopping a beating. When I spotted large game in the jungle—too large for me to handle on my own—I'd bark for the guards and the men to come with their guns. They kept the best meat, but the men and I got a little bit. It was better than nothing. I learned that if they were beating one of my men, I could fool them into thinking game was nearby. By the time they realized there was nothing there, I was long gone and the men were back to work.

But sometimes I was just too angry for tricks. Sometimes I went directly after the guards.

One day, one of my men dropped a tool down a small ravine. I was hiding in the jungle when I saw a guard start to beat him. I ran out of the bush and barked and snarled, standing between the guard and my man.

The guard raised his rifle.

"Go, girl!" Frank yelled.

I saw a flash and dodged out of the way just in time before dashing back into the jungle. The guard then turned his wrath on Frank, and I thought I might have to go back to help him. But after a couple of blows, the guard gave up.

It was hours before Frank thought it was safe to call me back again. I did my best to apologize. I dropped a rat in his lap and gave him my sorriest smile.

I'll be more careful, I promised. *I won't let them kill me to punish you.*

In March of 1945, we were moved to a new camp farther up the railway line. Every day, we had to risk our lives on a train commute across wobbly bridges and on the edges of steep cliffs and deep ravines.

The men worked in chest-high water to cut railway ties. Leeches covered their bodies. Rations were reduced and the guards forced the men to work faster and faster. Rest periods disappeared.

Every day, more and more men died. Frank and I were skeletons, surviving on a handful of rice per day. Hunting became too difficult. The rats had disappeared and I didn't have the energy to try to catch anything else. Everyone said that if Frank died, I would die, too, of a broken heart. And if I died, Frank would soon follow.

I'll do my best to keep you alive, my friend, and you do the same for me.

Twenty-five POWs in our new camp died in March. In April, the rations were cut again and our death rate more than tripled. Ten men died in one day. In May and June, things continued to get worse.

But not all the news was bad. In May, the POWs learned that Germany had surrendered and the war in Europe was over.

"Those soldiers will be heading here now that we've crushed the Germans," the men told each other. Once again they urged each other to hang on just a little longer. "Soon," they whispered. "Soon."

The news seemed to make the Japanese even more determined to finish the railway. At the same time, many men were assigned to dig trenches along the tracks.

"We're digging our own graves," they muttered.

By July 27, 1945, we had been working on the railway for a full year. Every day, there were signs that the Allies were coming. We saw their planes almost daily. But what were they doing? Did they know we were here? We needed more than the sight of a plane every afternoon. We needed them.

Down here, I wanted to bark at them. *We're down here and we need you.*

There were rumors that the Allies had taken back the skies and most of the Pacific Islands. Local Sumatrans started flashing their "V for Victory" signs right in front of the Japanese. Then in August, there was news on the radio of a powerful new American bomb dropped over Japan.

Every day, Frank and I kept each other alive.

Until the day we learned that I had been officially sentenced to death.

CHAPTER 10
"SHOOT THE DOG"

With the Allies so close to liberating us, the Japanese and Korean guards got even meaner. We had all been infected with lice from the moment we stepped into the jungle, but now—for some unknown reason—they suddenly decided it was time to rid the men and the camp of the annoying little creatures. Maybe they thought our liberators would treat them with respect if we were rescued in halfway decent condition. But given the fact that the men were mere skeletons, that seemed unlikely.

One day a few of the POWs were given razors, with orders to shave every head and every eyebrow. Others were tasked with burning all of the men's bedding and the rags that passed for clothing.

Then two of the guards squared off in front of Frank. He stiffened, and I sensed danger was near.

"Shoot the dog," ordered one of the guards to the other. "It's filthy and covered with lice." They both gave Frank big smiles. "We'll cook her—you'll eat the first bite."

"Disappear, Judy!" Frank yelled.

I could tell by the tone of his voice that he meant it, and I did, knowing that he would get a beating for warning me away.

For the next three days, rifle-carrying guards walked up and down the railway, whistling for me.

I'm not stupid enough to fall for your tricks! I thought.

I was too sneaky for them, but every once in a while, one of them thought they saw me and fired. I worried about what the sound of those guns would do to Frank. I was sure that every time he heard a gun go off, he thought I was dead. If it wasn't so dangerous, I would have crept into camp at night to let him know I was okay, but I couldn't.

They stopped looking one day when they discovered a tiger on their trail, but I still didn't think it was safe to return. Mostly I worried about Frank. Did he think I was dead? Was he giving up?

I'm alive, my friend, I wanted to tell him. *Just hang on. I'm okay, don't worry about me.*

I was hovering on the edge of the jungle late that third night when I heard quiet, sneaky noises. The guards were packing up and leaving! They slithered away like snakes in the dark. I waited until dawn to make sure they were really and truly gone, and then I ran into the center of camp.

Wake up! Wake up! I barked. *The kickers are gone!*

I was so happy I jumped around in circles, barking.

The prisoners slowly limped out of their huts, wondering what new horrors the Japanese were trying to inflict upon them and me. Instead, they found a camp empty of guards.

Frank ran over and I leaped upon him. We rolled around like we had when we were reunited at the camp in Singapore.

We're alive, and we're together! I barked.

A few minutes later, we heard the sound of an engine. I could tell that it was different from the Japanese trucks. I led the men into a clearing just beyond the camp, where we found two British soldiers sitting in a jeep.

"The war's over, mates," they told us. "The Japanese surrendered."

It was August 15, 1945. Men dropped to their knees, laughing and crying. They hugged each other and the British soldiers who had found us. I stayed by Frank's side, wagging my tail at these new friends.

"We're free!" someone shouted, and then all of the men picked up the cheer. "We're free! We're free!"

The war in the Pacific had lasted for 1,364 days. I had been a prisoner for most of it. And now I was finally free.

All that day and night, planes flew overhead, dropping parachutes with crates of food—real, wonderful food like meat, cheese, and eggs. There was chocolate and bread and butter and jam. And coffee. The men loved the coffee. (The yucky brown liquid had no appeal for me.)

At first the food made them sick, but slowly their bodies got used to being nourished again. Even I got a little queasy, but it was worth it for a full belly.

"Hey, you know something?" Frank said to me. "Now that this war is over, you can have your own rice ration. You don't need to share with me."

I thumped my tail in response. *And I don't have to catch any more rats.*

Clothing also came to us from the sky, which was a good thing because the men were all naked after the lice incident. Bedding, medical equipment, and even portable kitchens and bathrooms were parachuted from the sky.

The men were grateful, but what they really wanted was to go home.

"When?" they asked.

"Soon" was the reply.

Thankfully, that was the truth. After about a week, we

sailed to Singapore and went straight to the hospital. Frank was recovering from malaria, and we both needed to gain some weight.

Then there was talk of sending him home. Dogs weren't allowed on airplanes, so Frank refused to take one.

"I'll wait for a ship," he said. "I'm not leaving Judy."

Finally, after about a month in Singapore, we were playing catch one afternoon when a medical orderly handed Frank his embarkation papers.

"Here we go, girl," Frank said, reading the orders. "To leave for England aboard the troopship *Antenor*." Then his face crumpled. There was a footnote: "No dogs, birds, or pets of any kind to be taken aboard."

"I'm not leaving you behind, Judy," Frank whispered to me. "It's time for another smuggling operation."

I licked his hand to let him know that I understood.

I'm ready. Just tell me what to do.

On the day we were set to leave for England, Frank asked four of his friends to help. We strolled to the docks. I trailed behind, pretending to be a stray dog out for a walk. When we got close, I avoided the military police and slipped behind some duffel bags near the gangway.

I watched Frank board and show his papers to the two guards at the top of the gangway. I kept my eyes on him and waited.

Frank's friends walked up the gangway together a few minutes later and started a conversation with the guards. They kept pointing back at the city and pulled the guards away from the gangway to show them something. That's when Frank gave me the signal. It was a low whistle. The guards were too busy talking to hear it, but my super dog ears wouldn't miss that sound.

I scrambled up the gangway and into the duffel bag at Frank's feet. We'd done it again.

We're going to England!

Frank took me belowdecks, where I hid out with his gear.

Over the next six weeks, we relaxed and ate, and ate and relaxed. We let the ship's cook know early on that I was a stowaway, and he saved the best bones for me. By the time we neared Liverpool in England, Frank and I were both healthy again. I had forgotten how shiny and beautiful my coat could be.

Frank realized he was going to have to reveal his secret if I was going to make it ashore. Three days before we docked, he went to the captain and confessed. The captain was angry at first, but Frank told him all about me and how we'd kept each other alive. I went to visit him and gave him my prettiest smile. He radioed someone on shore and got permission for me to make landfall.

There was just one problem.

England said I had to stay in quarantine for six months to make sure I was healthy and wouldn't pass any nasty diseases to English animals.

Look at how beautiful I am, I wanted to tell them. *I'm healthy!*

I knew it. Frank knew it. But England couldn't be sure, and the officials wouldn't budge.

The ship anchored in Liverpool on October 29, 1945, and Frank had no choice but to hand me over to the Ministry of Agriculture. My new prison was a lot nicer than the prisons in Sumatra, and I didn't have to hunt for rats to survive. But my real home was with Frank, and I missed him.

He visited a lot, but it wasn't the same.

"You'll be home with me soon, girl," he'd promise every time he came.

Not soon enough for me, I thought.

Lots of other friends from Sumatra came to visit, too. It was good to see them all looking so fat and healthy.

Soon more and more people heard my story and wanted to visit. By the time I was released on April 29, 1946, all the dog lovers in England had heard Frank's and my story. I was made an official member of the Royal Air Force and even had my own uniform to match Frank's!

There was a big ceremony the day I got out, with lots of people taking pictures. Newspapers wrote stories about me, and I barked on the radio.

I'm famous! I thought. *And so is Frank!*

Crowds came to see me wherever I went, and I even spent some time with movie stars. But my favorite thing to do was visit children in hospitals. Small humans—with the exception of Frank, of course—are the best humans there are.

On July 22, 1946, Frank and I were both demobilized by the military. That meant we could go home to Portsmouth, where Frank lived before the war, and that's exactly what we did.

After everything we had been through, we were finally home. Together.

EPILOGUE

AFRICA

Frank and I were a man and dog of the world, and we soon became restless at home in England. Then, in 1948, Frank had a chance to travel to Africa for work. The first thing he did was check to make sure I could go along. When he got a yes, we made our plans. We got on an airplane—my very first plane ride—and flew to Tanganyika. Today, it's known as Tanzania, a country in Africa.

We spent our days in Frank's jeep, traveling from plantation to plantation and village to village for Frank's work. He was working with local farmers to cultivate crops like peanuts in the areas of Africa that were still part of Great Britain. My favorite thing to do was explore the bush. Africa had a lot of snakes and elephants like the ones I had seen in Sumatra, but there were new animals here I had never seen or smelled before, like lions and giraffes. The baboons reminded me too much of Mickey the monkey, so I did my best to avoid them.

We had been in Africa for a couple of years when something surprising happened. I was fourteen years old by then, and moving a little more slowly than I used to. One day I was out roving in the bush when I got lost. I didn't understand why. It had never happened before, but when dark came, I couldn't find my way home.

Before I knew it, there was a lion on my trail and I had to race away from it, and then I was even more turned around. There was no trace of Frank's scent, no trace of home. It took me a long time to find any humans at all.

I limped into a village a few days after I got lost. I knew Frank was looking for me, but I didn't know how to let him know where I was. My age made me too tired to search for him.

Luckily, Frank found me a couple of days after that and carried me home.

I felt okay after a bath, a big meal, and a good sleep. But a couple of nights later, on February 16, I woke up with a terrible pain. Frank tried to comfort me, but I could hardly walk. So Frank carried me in his arms once again, this time to the doctor.

I had surgery to remove a tumor that was causing the pain, but then an infection set in.

Frank came to sit with me with tears streaming down his cheeks. I knew what that meant. I had said goodbye to too many friends over the years. This would be the hardest one of all.

I licked his hand. *Goodbye, my friend.*

Then I fell asleep in the arms of my most special human. I was buried in my RAF jacket—the one that matched Frank's. I wouldn't have wanted it any other way.

HISTORICAL NOTE

Judy was a real dog who became the only animal to become an official prisoner of war during World War II. Although it's impossible to know what she was really thinking and feeling, all of the events in this novel really happened to the English pointer born in Shanghai in 1936.

Everyone who knew Judy said she had a remarkable ability to sense when danger was near. Somehow she knew the difference between who was an enemy and who was a friend even before she spent any time with them. And she was able to tell the difference between Japanese planes and ships, and those of friendly countries.

Many men who suffered as prisoners of war alongside Judy credit the dog with helping them stay alive. Not only did she distract guards from beatings and supply whatever food she could, Judy reminded the men of home. She lifted their spirits and gave them a reason to hang on.

Of course, not all of the men made it. An estimated 677 of the 6,000 POWs sent to work on the Death Railway died in Sumatra. The war took the lives of many, many more men, women, and children from all over the world.

Almost every country on earth took part in World War II. The United States, Great Britain, the Soviet Union, China, and other countries were on one side. They were called the Allies. Germany, Japan, and the countries that supported them were on the other. They were called the Axis powers.

The war between the Allied countries and the Axis powers lasted from September 1939 until August 1945. Many other animals took part in the war, helping their militaries just as Judy helped her men.

A NOTE ON PLACE NAMES

If you look on a map for some of the places Judy mentions during the course of her story, you won't find them. That's because many places are known by different names today. Below is a list of what they're called in this book, next to their current names.

DURING WWII	TODAY
Dutch East Indies	Indonesia
Hankow	Hankou
Nanking	Nanjing
Sawah Luento	Sawahlunto
Tanganyika	Tanzania

THE REAL-LIFE JUDY, POSING FOR PHOTOGRAPHERS AFTER RETURNING TO ENGLAND.

FOUR OF JUDY'S PUPPIES EXPLORE THE DECK OF THE GRASSHOPPER.

FRANK AND JUDY, PROUDLY SHOWING OFF HER DICKIN MEDAL.

JUDY LEARNED TO DODGE BICYCLES, CARS, AND FOOT TRAFFIC ON THE BUSY STREETS OF SHANGHAI.

PIRATES ATTEMPTED TO BOARD THE HMS *GNAT* IN AN ISOLATED GORGE LIKE THIS ONE ON THE YANGTZE RIVER.

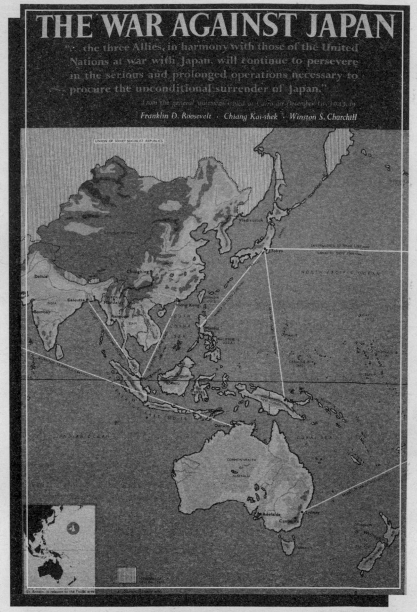

THE WAR AGAINST JAPAN

"...the three Allies, in harmony with those of the United Nations at war with Japan, will continue to persevere in the serious and prolonged operations necessary to procure the unconditional surrender of Japan."

From the general statement issued at Cairo on December 1st, 1943, by

Franklin D. Roosevelt · Chiang Kai-shek · Winston S. Churchill

JUDY SAILED FROM CHINA TO SINGAPORE ON THE HMS *GRASSHOPPER*. AFTER THE JAPANESE INVADED SINGAPORE AND THE *GRASSHOPPER* WAS SUNK, SHE SAILED TO SUMATRA WHERE SHE WAS TAKEN PRISONER.

JUDY BECAME MASCOT OF THE HMS *GRASSHOPPER* IN 1938.

FRANK AND JUDY SOMETIMES LIVED IN BARRACKS LIKE THIS ONE FROM A PRISONER-OF-WAR CAMP IN SINGAPORE.

THE SUMATRAN TIGER
IS A RARE AND DEADLY
SUBSPECIES FOUND
ONLY ON THE ISLAND OF
SUMATRA.

JUDY RECEIVED THE DICKIN
MEDAL, THE HIGHEST AWARD
ANY ANIMAL CAN RECEIVE, FOR
HER COURAGE AND FOR SAVING
LIVES IN THE JAPANESE
PRISON CAMPS.

JUDY WAS SURROUNDED BY FORMER PRISONERS OF WAR WHEN SHE RECEIVED THE DICKIN MEDAL ON MAY 2, 1946. FRANK IS STANDING TO HER RIGHT.

JUDY'S GRAVE IN TANZANIA, AFRICA READS: "IN MEMORY OF JUDY DM CANINE VC. BREED ENGLISH POINTER. BORN SHANGHAI FEBRUARY 1936. DIED FEBRUARY 1950. WOUNDED 14TH FEBRUARY 1942."

FURTHER READING

Want to read more about Judy, World War II, or other military animals? Check out these great books.

Bomb: The Race to Build—and Steal—the World's Most Dangerous Weapon by Steve Sheinkin, Flash Point. This is the story of the plotting, risk-taking, deceit, and genius that created the atomic bomb—the weapon that brought World War II to an end.

Dive! World War II Stories of Sailors & Submarines in the Pacific by Deborah Hopkinson, Scholastic. Read all about the heroic sailors aboard the US submarines who fought to stop the Japanese invasion across the Pacific.

Lost in the Pacific, 1942 by Tod Olson, Scholastic. This true story follows a group of soldiers who fought for survival at sea when a plane crash left them stranded in the middle of Japanese waters during World War II.

DK Eyewitness Books: World War II by Simon Adams, DK Children. Photographs, illustrations, documents, and maps tell the stories of the people, places, and events of World War II.

Military Animals by Laurie Calkhoven, Scholastic. Read about the dogs, horses, elephants, and even carrier pigeons that have aided soldiers through the ages.

No Better Friend: Young Readers Edition: A Man, a Dog, and Their Incredible True Story of Friendship and Survival in World War II by Robert Weintraub, Little, Brown Books for Young Readers. Read the nonfiction account of Judy's extraordinary life.

ABOUT THE AUTHOR

LAURIE CALKHOVEN spent her summer vacations on a farm in Iowa ruled over by a St. Bernard dog named Ginger. At home in New Jersey, Friskie (a mutt adopted from the dog pound) refused to be trained not to run into the road. Then she ran right into a moving car. Friskie got around on three legs after that, and learned not to play in traffic. There's no room for a dog in the New York City apartment where Laurie currently lives, but her nieces and nephews have four: Hudson, Meisje, Molly, and Lucy.

Laurie is the author of many books for young readers, including *Military Animals* and *Women Who Changed the World*.